the Rainstick
a fable

by

Sandra Chisholm Robinson,
Assistant Director, The Watercourse

Illustrations by
Peter Grosshauser

FALCONGUIDE®

GUILFORD, CONNECTICUT
HELENA, MONTANA

AN IMPRINT OF THE GLOBE PEQUOT PRESS

FALCONGUIDES®

Copyright © 1994 by Morris Book Publishing, LLC.
Previously published by Falcon Publishing, Inc. & The Watercourse

"Build Your Own Rainstick" illustrations by Laurie "gigette" Gould

Robinson, Sandra Chisholm.
     The rainstick: a fable / by Sandra Chisholm Robinson;
   illustrations by Peter Grosshouser.
        p. cm.
   Includes bibliographical references.
   Summary: A boy embarks on a quest to bring back the sound of rain to his West African village. Includes a discussion of how rainsticks are used today and instructions for making a rainstick.
     ISBN 978-1-56044-284-4
     [1. Rain and rainfall—Fiction. 2. Africa, West--Fiction.]
I. Grosshauser, Peter, ill. II. Title.
PZ7.R56758Rai 1994
[Fic]–dc20

                                        94-21587
                                          CIP
                                          AC

Printed in Korea
First Edition/Ninth Printing

About the Watercourse
The goal of The Watercourse is to promote and facilitate public understanding of atmospheric, surface and groundwater resources, and related management issues through publications, instruction, and networking. Currently, The Watercourse has two programs: The Watercourse Public Education Program for all water users and Project WET (Water Education for Teachers), co-sponsored with WREEC (Western Regional Environmental Education Council), for young people and educators.

The Watercourse
201 Culbertson Hall
Montana State University
Bozeman, MT 59717-0057
(406) 994–5392

the Rainstick

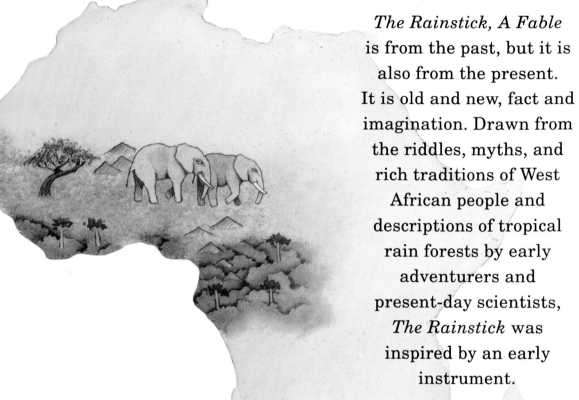

The Rainstick, A Fable is from the past, but it is also from the present. It is old and new, fact and imagination. Drawn from the riddles, myths, and rich traditions of West African people and descriptions of tropical rain forests by early adventurers and present-day scientists, *The Rainstick* was inspired by an early instrument.

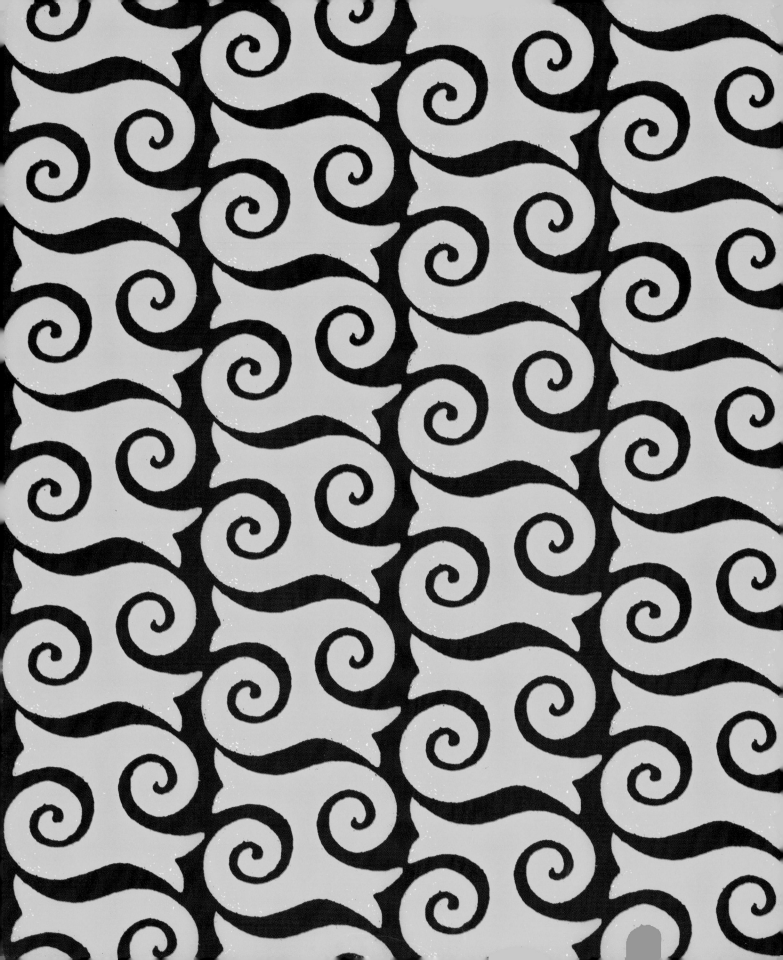

The Storyteller

The boy smiled as he dreamed of a great feast that flowed from a magic drum whenever he beat upon it. He smelled fragrant fufu, a creamy food made from yams, and licked his lips. But his tongue was rough on his dry, swollen lips and his stomach growled with hunger. The dream ended abruptly.

He opened his eyes and stared at the walls of his family's hut, dark from the smoke of many fires. He rolled over on his back and, holding his breath, listened anxiously. He waited until his chest ached and then with a gush the air rushed from him. No, the comforting rhythm of rain tapping on the roof was not to be heard.

The boy moved through the opening of the hut. Outside, he stretched and yawned like the lion after a morning nap

and anxiously searched the sky for rain clouds. But the blue reached unbroken to the line where sky and earth came together.

He dipped the hollowed-out gourd into the water jar by the door of the hut. The gourd scraped the bottom of the pot—scrunch, scrunch. He thought, my mother must still be at the river getting water.

The boy remembered how the river once flowed freely and murmured its happy song. In his mind he sees a small boy splashing a woman. Her laughter is like the sound of little bells. She stops rinsing her clothes at the river's edge and dashes into the shallow water. She gathers the boy up and hugs him tightly. As she spins in a circle, he throws open his arms and leans back to look at the sky . . .

6

Remembering how good the water felt the boy raised his hand to wipe the water drops from his face. But his smooth, dark skin was dry and hot from the relentless sun.

The boy heard the laughter of women as they passed his hut. They were on their way to tend the crops in the fields. But their laughter was not like tiny bells; it was cruel and harsh and punctuated with words that pierced like the spear. He turned his back to them, but the words still found their mark. The women spoke of his father.

His father was a leader in the village; he was the rain-maker. When the boy was small, each year the good rain had come in its time. Green and robust, seedlings burst from the earth and under the ground the yams ripened full and sweet. Babies grew round with their mother's rich milk.

The people feasted. Laughter, singing, dancing, and storytelling filled the village. The river flowed full between its banks and added its voice to the people's happiness.

But the clouds that brought the rain no longer visited the sky above the village. The sun was hot and the winds dry. Now the seedlings struggled through the hard baked earth. For a while, the people did not worry; they carried water from the river to relieve the thirst of their plants. But the river's voice grew quieter as less water flowed between its banks. Now the river no longer flowed, but pooled in muddy, shrinking puddles.

Like the elephant that digs for water in dry times, the people dug in places that had once held water. But only dry sand trickled through their fingers. Even his father's rain stones had been unsuccessful in bringing the rain.

On his way to the river, the boy walked the long way through the huts of the village. He passed by the hut of the storyteller. The old man raised his hand and beckoned to him. The boy liked the old man. Although his hair was white and his back stooped, his thin wiry body was still strong. The storyteller had seen many places and knew many things.

He told of kings and kingdoms that had great streets,

broad and very long. The streets were lined with many houses that were connected to each other. The houses had several rooms and courtyards. In the palace of the king, the storyteller saw gates upon gates that passed into other places. The king had many soldiers and servants who carried water, yams, and the drink of the palm. And the king's stable was filled with horses, their necks proudly arched and their coats glistening in the sunlight.

The people of the village frequently begged the storyteller to speak of the markets. He would smile and patiently recite the exotic goods he had seen: a cloth that flowed like water and was woven with many colors, stone and glass beads, fragrant spices with smells that made a person's mouth water, and shells from the ocean.

The boy paused before entering the storyteller's hut. He remembered past nights of the whole moon, when the people gathered in the center of the village after their work was done. Talking gaily, the women balanced their babies on their hips and traded bits of gossip. After sipping the drink of the palm tree, the men gathered before the blazing fire. Jostling for the best seats, small children hurried to fill in the spaces. When all was ready, the people asked for the storyteller.

The storyteller walked slowly into the circle and sat on his small, finely carved stool. He did not speak. He studied his eager audience. Sometimes his dark eyes would twinkle like the stars and the little children would squirm with anticipation. "A riddle," the older ones said. "Listen, the storyteller will give us a riddle."

In a strong, clear voice the old man said, "I have two brothers and sisters and cannot see either of them." The people wrinkled their foreheads as they pondered their answers. The boy had been very young on the night when he responded, "My ears and eyes are my brothers and sisters." His father and mother had been proud of him.

Clearing his thoughts, the boy joined the storyteller in his hut. A fire burned and the acrid smoke made his eyes water.

The storyteller did not look at him for a long time. The old man studied the flames of the fire and watched the tendrils of smoke rise like ghostly snakes to the thatched roof of his hut. He looked briefly at the boy and then, having made up his mind, removed the pouch from around his neck. He held it in his clenched, gnarled fist close to his chest.

Signaling for the boy to open his hand, the storyteller laid the pouch gently on his flat palm.

11

The boy waited patiently until the storyteller nodded his head. Then he reached into the pouch and slowly withdrew a single, perfect feather. It was blue but in the firelight reflected many colors.

The storyteller said simply, "This feather belongs to the bird that lives in the place of rain. There must be great power where this bird lives, for the rain visits every day. The trees grow so tall they hide the sun."

The boy looked in wonder at the old man.

The storyteller paused and then continued. "Perhaps if a man journeyed to this place where the bird lives, he could return to his village with the sound of the rain."

"In what direction would a man travel to find the home of this bird?" the boy asked.

The storyteller rose slowly to his feet and moved to the door of his hut. He motioned for the boy to join him. Stretching out his arm, the old man pointed to where the river, slender as a thread, joined the dark blue line of the horizon. "That is where a man would go."

"That is not so far," said the boy brightly. "A man could walk there and return in the same day."

The storyteller was silent.

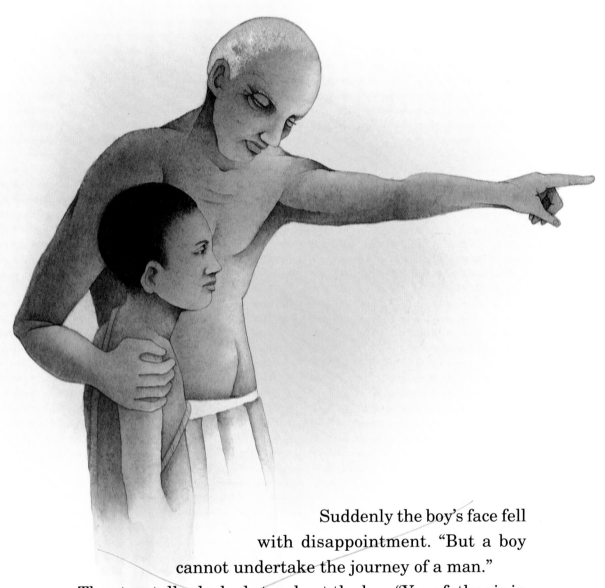

Suddenly the boy's face fell
with disappointment. "But a boy
cannot undertake the journey of a man."
The storyteller looked sternly at the boy. "Your father is in
danger. There is little food left in the village. As the people's
hunger grows, so does their fear and anger. They spit bitter
words at him now, but the words may turn to blows. The
sound of the rain must soon return to the village."

Holding back the tears of fear and pain, the boy slowly nodded his head and turned to go.

"Wait," the storyteller said, "a riddle . . . . A slender staff touches earth and sky at the same time."

The boy wrinkled his brow and shook his head.

"Carry this riddle with you on your journey—it will not weigh much." The storyteller watched as the troubled boy followed the path through the village.

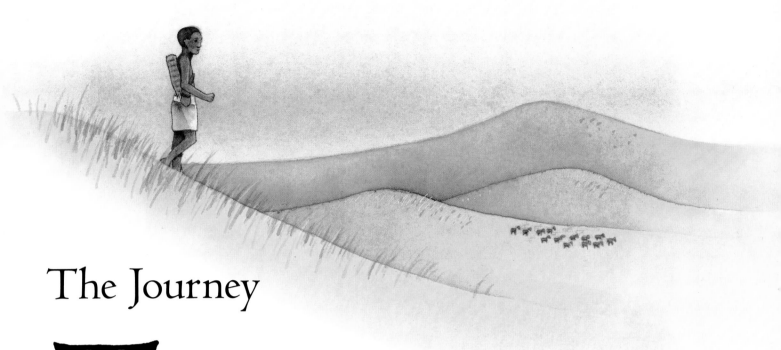

The Journey

The boy had been pursuing the horizon for many suns. Sometimes he grew angry and frustrated, thinking the storyteller must have tricked him. The line where the sky and the earth came together never seemed any closer.

The land through which the boy passed was like his homeland. The brown, prickly stubble poked through the sides of his flat sandals. He woke early and walked until the heat of the day made him see shimmering things that weren't really there.

On a day when he had not found water, he saw his mother. As her image wavered in the heat, she held out a calabash from which sparkling water flowed. He ran toward her, but after a few steps the heat brought him to his knees. When he looked up, she had vanished. After that he rested in the shade

of a large rock or tree during the heat of the day and traveled when the sun was lower in the sky.

At night he searched for a tree in which to sleep. One evening as the sky was tinted purple and gold, he selected a baobab tree. His people called it the upside-down tree, for the twisted web of branches looked like roots. The trunk was thick and scarred by elephants that gouged the wood with their tusks for its precious water. The boy picked the green fuzzy fruit that hung from a long stem. He pounded it on a rock until the fruit cracked open. He dug out the seeds and sucked the white powder that surrounded them. He savored the sour, tangy flavor and finally spit out the brown seeds.

The next morning he woke to find a pride of lions resting at the base of the baobab. The boy remembered a tale from the storyteller of a man who understood the language of the animals. The boy talked quietly to the lions and showing them the storyteller's feather asked if they knew of the place of the rain.

The lions were full after a night of hunting and only perked their ears at the sounds made by the boy. They lazily swatted insects with their tails and the mothers licked their cubs with rough tongues.

The boy waited patiently in the tree until the lions wandered off. Finally, he too renewed his journey.

One day he was fortunate enough to come upon the nests of the large birds that sometimes roared like lions. The boy was only half as tall as the birds. Their eggs were of great size. When a bird left its nest to feed, the boy quickly snatched an egg. He cracked it open. The runny insides tasted good.

As the distance between the boy and the village grew, the land changed. The grass grew thicker, greener, and taller. He did not have to search so hard for a tree to sleep in at night. The boy sometimes saw large villages, but because he was a stranger, he did not enter them.

Water became easier to find. Like the other small animals he waited his turn at the water holes while the elephants, lions, and the silent giraffes drank. Birds swooped in great flocks to sip from the pools, the blue waters muddied by the herds.

The boy fished in the rivers. Where the waters were very low, the fish were trapped in small pools and he easily scooped them up with his fish weir. But his fishing was not carefree. He was always watchful of the grinning crocodile and the hippopotamus that jealously guarded its territory.

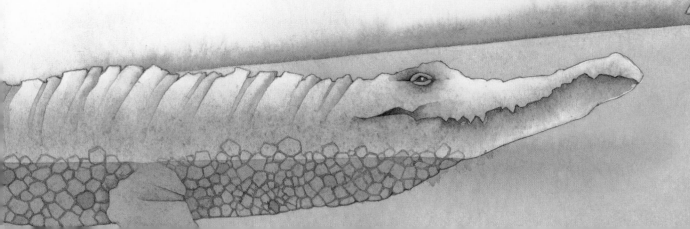

Although he now suffered neither hunger nor thirst, the boy worried about the many suns that had come and gone. His absence was likely another burden for his father and mother to bear. Perhaps the rains had come, but in the part of himself that was always connected to his people he knew they had not.

At first light of the new day, the boy walked through the tall grass. He saw something which broke the line between the earth and the sky. He moved toward it. It was a gently rounded mountain; he could climb it. Perhaps he could see the way to the land of the rain.

From the top of the mountain, he surveyed the country before him. In the distance was a forest—he had found the place of the rain.

It took two more suns to reach the great trees. The boy waded through low shrubby plants that stroked his waist and legs. He approached the strange forest slowly. He felt a pounding in his chest, his breath came quickly. His mouth was so dry he couldn't spit.

The storyteller had told tales of this feeling—people who faced leopards felt it. The boy turned his thoughts from himself to the thirsty villagers . . . to the storyteller . . . to his father and mother. Now he drew strength from his fear.

He approached the great trees. He thought, I am like the ant to the elephant!

Inside, the forest was moist and comforting unlike the glare of the hot, white sun. The boy leaned his head back and looked into the mass of branches and leaves that seemed to grow into the sky. Sometimes the sun broke through the leaves that grew at the very tops of the trees and drew patterns on the forest floor. The floor was littered with sticks, leaves, and the remains of fruit that had fallen or had been dropped by animals foraging in the tree tops.

He picked up a piece of discarded fruit, smelled it and then took a tiny bit. He chewed it slowly and swallowed. He waited to see what his stomach thought. Feeling no cramps, he shrugged and ate the whole thing. After he finished, he licked the sweet juice from each finger.

As the light became softer in the forest, he knew he must find a place to sleep. He found a tree with rough gray bark like the skin of the elephant. The boy thought it must be a grandfather tree; many people holding hands in a circle could not reach around it. Grasping a vine the size of a man's arm, the boy climbed up. A wide lower branch formed a shelf close to the great trunk. Here the boy curled up and waited for sleep.

In the growing darkness, the sounds of the forest pressed closer to the boy. Shrill screams and gentle cooing filled the damp night. Insects whined and buzzed. Occasionally he heard the low rumble from the throat of a stalking leopard or the shrieks of quarreling monkeys.

But it was another sound that caused the boy's heart to beat painfully in his chest. The moist air of the forest carried the voices of talking drums.

The Bird

The next morning the boy followed a well-worn path. Often he stopped to rest, for breathing the damp air was tiring for him. Yet, for a child of the open plains he adjusted quickly to the low light, the rich greens and browns of the forest with the rare flush of red of new leaves and the continual voices of the birds. Only the occasional snake dropping from the trees to the path in front of him, was a reminder that he was a stranger in a foreign land.

The boy stopped to listen to the call of a bird he did not know. Without warning the rain came. For a long time he stood still. He closed his eyes and felt the soaking rain and rejoiced with a song of his people.

The rain fell gently, but steadily, in the forest and the boy decided to take shelter. Close to the path he found a large tree; at its base, roots overlapped.

He rested in the protection of the massive tree and listened to the sound of the rain. He imagined single drops sliding down large, leathery leaves, suspended for an instant at the green tips and then falling like tears to the damp ground. Like the cradlesongs mothers hum to their babies, the song of the rain comforted the boy. He thought longingly of his home.

The rain turned to a fine mist. He dozed. Suddenly he was awakened by the distinct call of a bird. "Akoru-toku-toku-toku."

On the ground was the most beautiful bird the boy had ever seen. Even in the low light of the forest its feathers reflected the color of sky and water. The boy moved his hand to the pouch that hung around his neck; he traced the shaft of the storyteller's feather inside. He did not have to look. He knew the feather had come from a bird like this one.

The bird moved quickly and nervously in the boy's direction. It cocked its head to the side and looked at the boy with a bright eye. Then it turned and flew a few feet away. The bird repeated these movements several times. Finally the boy said to the bird, "I think you want me to follow you."

The rain had stopped and the forest smelled of rich earth. The bird flew a few feet ahead of him and the boy followed. Although the bird always remained just out of the boy's reach, it never allowed him to fall too far behind.

Finally the bird broke into a clearing and landed on a high wall. The boy gasped. They had come to a village. Suddenly the bird threw back its head and sang in a beautiful voice. The boy was afraid; a villager might see him. He picked up a rock and thought to silence the bird. But as he did, the bird's song entered the boy's heart. He lowered his arm and the stone fell to the ground.

From the other side of the wall the boy heard the noises of the villagers. Of all their sounds, he only recognized one—laughter.

The bird stopped its singing. In a blur of green and blue it was gone. Suddenly the boy felt alone. He withdrew to the forest, but stayed close enough to hear the comforting sounds of the village.

That night, as he rested in a large tree, he listened for the people. He heard the sounds of singing, dancing, and the voices of drums. But there was also a new sound; he leaned forward and strained to hear. Yes, it was the gentle sound of

27

rain. He looked up; through a break in the forest cover the light of the moon shone. Although the boy could hear its voice, no rain fell from the sky.

He shivered. What a wonderful and powerful people. They had captured the sound of rain.

The next morning the boy woke to a great noise in the forest. The birds in the tree tops did not sing with their beautiful morning voices, but shrieked with harsh, raucous calls of alarm. Pounding the tree branches and lashing the leaves, the monkeys screamed. For a long time the boy cowered close to the trunk of the tree until finally the forest was quiet. It was as if a great and terrible storm had passed.

The boy slid down the tree. Today he would go to the village.

The mist was heavy in the forest; like walking through a cloud he thought. But nothing moved; nothing spoke.

Approaching the village the boy sensed that the people were gone. He scaled the wall and dropped down on the other side. The village had many huts that were shaped differently from the ones he knew.

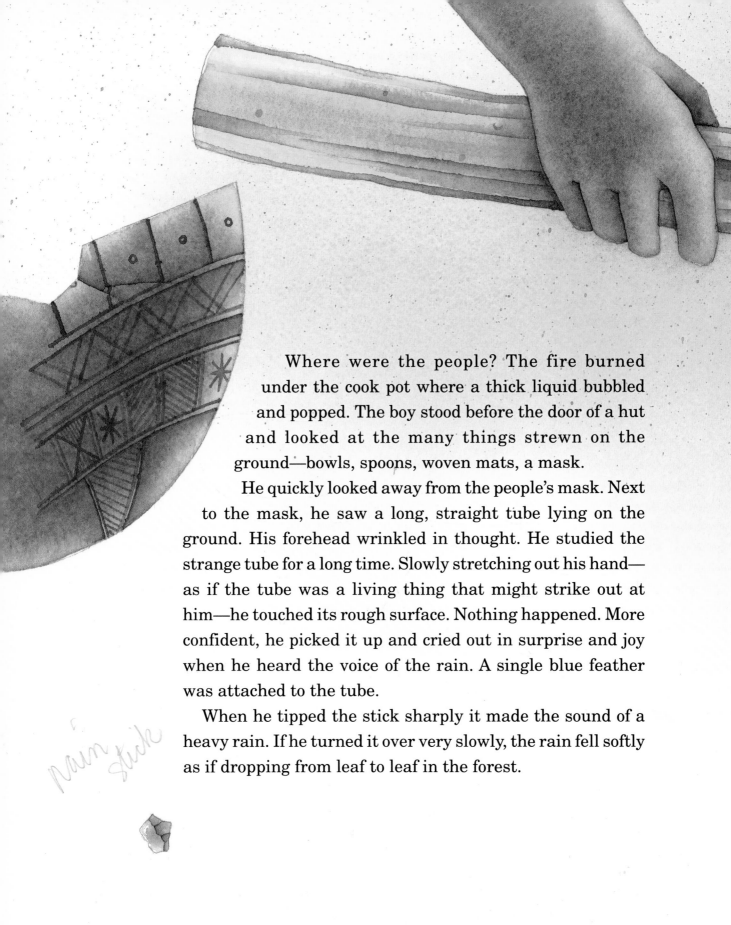

rain stick

Where were the people? The fire burned under the cook pot where a thick liquid bubbled and popped. The boy stood before the door of a hut and looked at the many things strewn on the ground—bowls, spoons, woven mats, a mask.

He quickly looked away from the people's mask. Next to the mask, he saw a long, straight tube lying on the ground. His forehead wrinkled in thought. He studied the strange tube for a long time. Slowly stretching out his hand—as if the tube was a living thing that might strike out at him—he touched its rough surface. Nothing happened. More confident, he picked it up and cried out in surprise and joy when he heard the voice of the rain. A single blue feather was attached to the tube.

When he tipped the stick sharply it made the sound of a heavy rain. If he turned it over very slowly, the rain fell softly as if dropping from leaf to leaf in the forest.

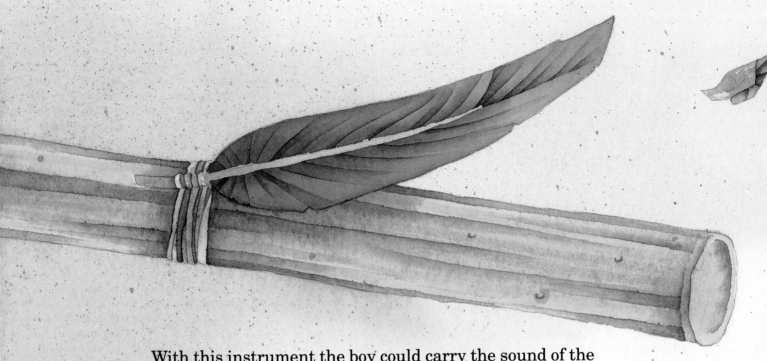

With this instrument the boy could carry the sound of the rain back to his village. He looked around. He could not just take the instrument; he fingered the bag that hung around his neck. The storyteller's pouch had been a great comfort to the boy on his journey. He removed it from around his neck and placed it at the door of the hut. He could not have known that the bag would mold and rot in the damp heat of the forest. The people of this village would never return.

Turning his face toward home, the boy followed the path through the forest. He would take back to his village the sound of the rain and stories of the place that the rain visited. Surely, his father would be spared.

Glancing at the rainstick, he thought of the riddle the storyteller had given him. "A slender staff touches earth and sky at the same time." The boy smiled and to the trees, the snakes, the insects, the leopard, he said, "It is the rain . . . the slender staff that touches earth and sky is the rain."

tip haenslich   *sound*

As the boy tipped the rainstick, its voice blended with the song
of the rain and the forest . . . in time with his hurrying steps.

About the Rainstick

The rainstick is a type of tubular rattle, a sound-producing instrument that belonged to the earliest cultures. Originally, many sound-producing instruments served ritual or magical purposes. Later they were used by adults for entertainment and finally were passed on to children for their amusement. Today, the rainstick is made and played by children in Cameroon and Liberia.

People continue to use the rainstick in different ways. In some parts of the world it has cultural meaning as a traditional instrument associated with the onset of rain and in other places it is simply played as a percussion instrument.

The rainstick is a hollow tube with an unusual internal structure. This matrix formed of cactus spines, wooden pegs, bamboo or palm slivers distinguishes the rainstick from other tube rattles. The cylinder is filled with pebbles, hard seeds, beans, sand, rice, or tiny shells. The ends of the tube are sealed. The rattle may be decorated with paint and feathers or sheathed with a woven cover.

Echoed in the quality of the sound it produces, the rainstick is a product of the environment in which it is found. Rain forest people create rainsticks from bamboo or the midrib of a raphia palm frond. A section of the center stem is cut from the palm frond, split lengthwise and hollowed out. Material is left at each end of the tube so that the ends are closed. The tube is filled with rice and fastened together with palm slivers.

The palm rainstick imitates the timbre of rain in the forest. Grains of rice tapping against each other, the pegs, and the sides of the tube create the muted sounds of raindrops on ferns, leaves, and the damp forest floor. In desert communities rainsticks have been constructed from various species of cactus.

The sound produced by a rainstick is determined by the material from which the tube is constructed, its length and circumference, the tiny objects enclosed, and the position of the internal needles. The needles or pegs may bisect the tube or only extend halfway through, like the spokes in a wheel. Rainsticks three to four feet long and two to three inches across were collected from the Kpelle and Loma peoples in rural areas of Liberia.

The way in which the rainstick is "played" affects its sound. Sometimes the tube is shaken like a rhythm instrument. The angle at which the stick is held determines not only the quality but also the duration of the sound.

Some musicologists believe that the rattle evolved in different parts of the world at the same time. Made from bamboo and similar in construction, a tubular rattle with pegs is found in Northern China.

Tubular rattles have also been discovered among people in South America. Other musicologists believe that the rainstick was developed in Africa and was introduced to South America by African peoples who were enslaved and carried by ships to this foreign continent. The rainstick is found sporadically throughout West Africa (i.e., South Togo, Liberia, Cameroon) in areas where slavers raided villages and patrolled forest trails.

The landscape of West Africa provides a hauntingly beautiful backdrop for *The Rainstick, A Fable*. The hot, dry grassland of the savanna contrasts sharply with the misty rain forests closer to the coast.

Legends, riddles, and customs reveal a people who knew that rain brought life, and drought, death. During periods of little or no rain, pasture lands turned brown and cattle and wild animals died—their bones bleached white by the hot sun. Rivers dried up, crops withered, and people died; villages were deserted. Some groups moved from the savanna to the rain forest in search of wetter places.

In some parts of West Africa the village leader was the rainmaker. As long as the harvest was good, the people gave the leader gifts. But when there was drought or flood the rainmaker was held responsible and might be insulted by his people or even harmed if weather conditions did not improve.

It is not surprising that a people intimately connected with the cycles of wet and dry created an instrument that imitated the sound of rainfall. But why are we attracted to the rainstick? Perhaps it is the pleasing sound, beautiful in its simplicity. Perhaps we are drawn to the rainstick because it connects us with different cultures and unfamiliar environments. Regardless of our attempts to explain its appeal, the rainstick brings together people of all ages and traditions in their delight and fascination with it.

Build Your Own Rainstick

As people build rainsticks from materials found in the environments in which they live, you too can create your own rainstick with things available within your home.

What you'll need

Cardboard tubes from paper towels or gift wrapping, mailing tubes
A tool to punch holes in the tube, such as a drill or awl
Small hammer
Toothpicks or **flat head nails** (1 inch diameter tube, 7/8 inch nail)
Glue
Masking tape
Wire cutters or **sturdy scissors**
"Fill" seeds, pebbles, rice, dried beans, shells, beads and so forth.
Materials to decorate the outside of the tube:
paint, crayons, sparkles, sand, etc.

The Steps

1. Drill or poke holes in the cardboard tube. Be careful not to collapse the tube by pressing too hard. Creating a spiral staircase pattern, place the holes about one inch apart. Drill the holes through one side only or all the way through both sides of the tube. If you are using nails, it is not necessary to drill holes.

2. Push the toothpicks through the holes. Leave a little bit of the toothpick (a nub) remaining outside the tube. If holes were drilled straight through the cylinder, push the toothpick all the way through the tube. Inserting the toothpicks to different lengths will produce a variety of sounds.

If you are using nails, insert nails that are slightly shorter than the diameter of the tube in a spiral pattern. A small hammer may be useful.

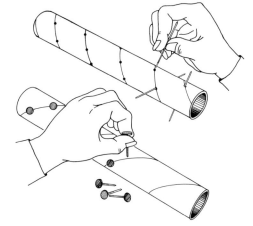

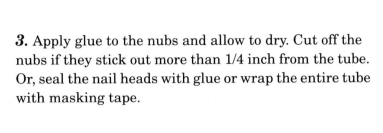

3. Apply glue to the nubs and allow to dry. Cut off the nubs if they stick out more than 1/4 inch from the tube. Or, seal the nail heads with glue or wrap the entire tube with masking tape.

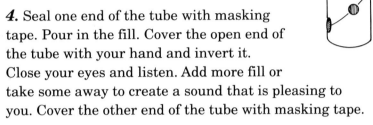

4. Seal one end of the tube with masking tape. Pour in the fill. Cover the open end of the tube with your hand and invert it. Close your eyes and listen. Add more fill or take some away to create a sound that is pleasing to you. Cover the other end of the tube with masking tape.

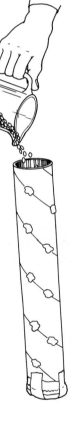

5. You may wish to decorate your rainstick by coating it with glue and rolling it in sand. (Messy, but it provides a wonderful texture for the surface of your instrument.) After it dries, you may paint and decorate it with natural objects from your own part of the world. Be creative!

When you slowly turn your rainstick end to end, listen for the sound of the rain. What stories do you hear?

37

Acknowledgments

The Watercourse appreciates the commitment and hard work of staff members who contributed to *The Rainstick, A Fable:*

Researchers: Chris McRae and George Robinson

Rainstick Design: Michael Brody

"Build Your Own Rainstick" written by: Jennie Lane

Reviewers: Dennis Nelson, Linda Hveem, Nancy Carrasco, Al Kesselheim, Kate McLean

The following individuals shared their knowledge of and/or experiences in West Africa, provided suggestions for resources and illustrations, or read the text for accuracy:

J. Kenneth Moore, Associate Curator, Department of Musical Instruments, Metropolitan Museum of Art

Dr. Cynthia Schmidt, Ethnomusicologist, Consultant

Bill Sigmund, Curator of the Arts of Africa, the Pacific and the Americas, The Brooklyn Museum

Françoise Djibode, born and raised in Benin, currently a graduate student at Montana State University

Teresa Galli, a Peace Corps volunteer in Africa, currently living in Bozeman, Montana

Verification of Adinkra motif: Dr. Joanne B. Eicher, Professor, Department of Design, Housing and Apparel, University of Minnesota

Mimi Games, Library Technician, National Museum of African Art, Smithsonian Institution

Vicki Rovine, Assistant Curator of the Arts of Africa, the Pacific and the Americas, The Brooklyn Museum

Special thanks to the Bureau of Reclamation.

With appreciation for the help of the Reference and Interlibrary Loan staff of the Montana State University Library, the staff of the Bozeman Public Library and the Lewis and Clark Library.

Peter Grosshauser extends his appreciation to the Ward family and to his technical assistant, Debbie Epperson.

The Watercourse thanks the Falcon Press staff who published *The Rainstick, A Fable* with great care and skill: Kathy Springmeyer, Project Manager; Megan Hiller, Editor; Jeff Wincapaw, Designer.

Bibliography

Books:

Arkhurst, Joyce Cooper. *The Adventures of Spider, West African Folk Tales*. Boston: Little, Brown and Company, 1964.*

Arnott, Kathleen. *African Myths and Legends*. Oxford: Oxford University Press, 1979.

Balandier, Georges and Jacques Maquet. *Dictionary of Black African Civilization*. New York: Leon Amiel, 1974.

Bannerman, David A. *Larger Birds of West Africa*. London: Penguin Books, 1958.

Bascom, William R. and Melville J. Herskovits. *Continuity and Change in African Cultures*. Chicago: The University of Chicago Press, 1959.

Bryson, Reid A. and Thomas J. Murray. *Climates of Hunger*. Madison: The University of Wisconsin Press, 1977.

Burton, Robert. *Animal Life*. New York: Oxford University Press, 1991.

Chinery, Michael. *Grassland Animals, A Random House TELL ME ABOUT Book*. New York: Random House, 1991.*

Davidson, Basil and the editors of Time-Life Books. *African Kingdoms*. New York: Time Incorporated, 1966.

De La Rue, Sidney. *The Land of the Pepper Bird, Liberia*. New York: G.P. Putnam's Sons, 1930.

Denslow, Julie Sloan and Christine Padoch. *People of the Tropical Rain Forest*. Los Angeles: University of California Press, 1988.

Fraginals, Manuel Moreno (ed.). *Africa in Latin America*. New York: Holmes and Meier Publishers, Inc., 1984.

Frazer, Sir James George. *The Golden Bough*. New York: Collier Books, 1963.

Hunter, C. Bruce. *Tribal Map of Negro Africa*. New York: The American Museum of Natural History, 1956.

Izikowitz, Karl Gustav. *Musical and Other Sound Instruments of the South American Indians, A Comparative Ethnographical Study.* Goteborg: Elanders Boktryckeri Aktiebolag, 1934.

Jablow, Alta. *The Intimate Folklore of Africa*. New York: Horizon Press, 1961.

Knappert, Jan. *Kings, Gods & Spirits from African Mythology*. New York: Peter Bedrick Books, 1986.*

Linsenmaier, Walter. *Insects of the World*. New York: McGraw-Hill Book Company, 1972.

Martin, Claude. *The Rain Forests of West Africa: Ecology/Threats/Conservation.* Boston: Birkhäuser Verlag, 1991.

Menninger, Edwin A. *Flowering Trees of the World.* New York: Hearthside Press Incorporated, 1962.

Menninger, Edwin A. *Edible Nuts of the World.* Stuart, Florida: Horticultural Books, Inc., 1977.

Murdock, George Peter. *Africa, Its Peoples and Their Culture History.* New York: McGraw-Hill Book Company, Inc., 1959.

Nketia, J.H. Kwabena. *The Music of Africa.* New York: W.W. Norton and Company, 1974.

Oliver, Roland and J.D. Fage. *A Short History of Africa.* New York: Penguin Books. 1990

Ottenberg, Simon and Phoebe. *Cultures and Societies of Africa.* New York: Random House, 1968.

Page, Jake. *Zoo: The Modern Ark.* New York: Facts on File, 1990.

Polakoff, Claire. *Into Indigo; African Textiles and Dyeing Techniques.* New York: Anchor Press, Doubleday, 1980.

Radin, Paul and Elinore Marvel. *African Folktales and Sculpture.* New York: Pantheon Books Inc., 1953.

Sachs, Curt. *Geist Und Werden Der Musikinstrumente.* Hilversum: Frits A. M. Knuf, 1965.

Sachs, Curt. *The History of Musical Instruments.* New York: W.W. Norton and Company, Inc., 1940.

Seabrook, William B. *Jungle Ways.* New York: Harcourt, Brace & Company, Inc., 1931.

Serle, William and Gérard J. Morel. *A Field Guide to the Birds of West Africa.* St. James Place, London: Collins, 1977.

Silverberg, Robert. *The World of the Rain Forest.* New York: Meredith Press, 1967.

Steward, Julian H. (ed.). *Handbook of South American Indians.* Washington, D.C.: United States Government Printing Office, 1946.

Whitmore, T.C. *An Introduction to Tropical Rain Forests.* Oxford: Clarendon Press, 1990.

Journals:

Von Hornbostel, E.M. "The Ethnology of African Sound Instruments" in *Journal of the International Institute of African Languages and Cultures.* Vol. VI, No. 2, April 1933.

*Indicates books for young readers.